*For Silvia Webb*

*Thank you for your love, inspiration, and
caring for my most precious treasure.*

Henry Holt and Company, *Publishers since 1866*
Henry Holt® is a registered trademark of Macmillan Publishing Group, LLC
120 Broadway, New York, NY 10271 • mackids.com

Library of Congress Cataloging-in-Publication Data
Names: Slack, Michael H., 1969- author, illustrator.
Title: Dragon meets Boy / Michael Slack.
Description: First edition. | New York : Henry Holt Books, 2020. | "Christy Ottaviano Books."
Audience: Ages 4-8. | Audience: Grades K-1.
Summary: A toy dragon and his human boy continue to share adventures, even after the boy grows up.
Identifiers: LCCN 2019039529 | ISBN 978-1-62779-271-4 (hardcover)
Subjects: CYAC: Toys—Fiction. | Dragons—Fiction. | Friendship—Fiction.
Adventure and adventurers—Fiction. | Imagination—Fiction. | Growth—Fiction.
Classification: LCC PZ7.S628832 Dr 2020 | DDC [E]—dc23
LC record available at https://lccn.loc.gov/2019039529

Our books may be purchased in bulk for promotional, educational, or business use.
Please contact your local bookseller or the Macmillan Corporate and Premium Sales Department at
(800) 221-7945 ext. 5442 or by email at MacmillanSpecialMarkets@macmillan.com.

First edition, 2020
The illustrations for this book were digitally painted and collaged in Adobe Photoshop.
Printed in China by Toppan Leefung Printing Ltd., Dongguan City, Guangdong Province

1 3 5 7 9 10 8 6 4 2

# Dragon Meets Boy

## Michael Slack

Christy Ottaviano Books

Henry Holt and Company ✦ New York

One summer day a dragon met a boy.
They were instant friends.

They had many amazing adventures.
Dragon showed Boy a world beyond the clouds.

They explored mysterious lands,
where creatures lurked in the shadows.

They scaled tall mountains

and battled the forces of evil.

When Boy was sad,
Dragon cheered him up.

When Boy was scared,
Dragon made him
feel brave.

WELCOME
to ROOM 9

Dragon was always by Boy's side.

H.A. REY · *Curious George* · H.M. CO.

SENDAK · WHERE THE WILD THINGS ARE · HARPER & ROW

Easton · ROBOTS YOU CAN BUILD · PW Press

Things changed. As Boy grew taller,
Dragon stayed the same size.

Boy went adventuring on his own.
Dragon was left behind.

Boy always came back, and Dragon was there when Boy needed him.

One evening Boy was preparing for his most important adventure. "I have found you the perfect cave," said Boy.

"These are my treasures. You must guard them while I'm away."

Boy put Dragon in the cave.
Dragon gave Boy one last hug.
Then it was goodbye.

There Dragon sat, protecting Boy's most precious things. When the treasure fell over, Dragon would stack it back up.

When it grew dull, Dragon would make it shine.

It was beautiful when it shined.

The treasure reminded him of Boy. It made him miss Boy.
Does Boy miss me? he wondered.

Days became years.

As time passed, Dragon grew more
and more weary . . .

. . . until finally he fell into a deep dragon sleep. He dreamed about Boy. He dreamed about adventure. He dreamed about . . .

the sun.

Rivers of light flooded the cave, waking up Dragon. A hand reached in and took one of Boy's most precious things. I must protect Boy's treasure, thought Dragon.

The thief returned again and again, each time
stealing another of Boy's treasures . . .

. . . until nothing was left. Dragon felt
like a failure. He had let Boy down.

Just then the thief grabbed Dragon. He flared his nostrils and wrapped his body around the thief's hand, twisting tighter and tighter. He was about to shoot a ball of fire as the thief pulled Dragon out of the cave.

Dragon was surprised. The thief was a child—a girl. All of Boy's treasures were there on the grass. He was even more surprised when he saw who was behind the girl.

It was Boy!

He looked different, but Dragon recognized him right away.

"Thank you for protecting my treasures," said Boy. "You are a brave and loyal friend." Dragon was happy that Boy had returned.

One spring day a dragon met a girl.
They were instant friends.
    Together they set out on the adventure
of a lifetime.